The FurFins

If you tiptoe to the shore
and gaze out at the sea,
you might just spot a sparkly tail
or a friendly furry face.
You've just seen a FurFin and found
a very special place.

Shhh, FurFins are real . . .

The FurFins
and the
Sparkly Sleepover

ALISON RITCHIE

illustrated by
ALESS BAYLIS

BLOOMSBURY
CHILDREN'S BOOKS

NEW YORK LONDON OXFORD NEW DELHI SYDNEY

Deep beneath the silvery waves,
nestled in a kaleidoscope of colorful coral,
lies the magnificent kingdom of Coralia.
This is where the FurFins live.

Look—there's StarTail and her seahorse Shine . . .

StarTail is so excited!
She's invited her friends
for a sleepover.

"Hurray! You're here!" she exclaimed as TinyTail and CherryTail
arrived with their seahorses Boo and Yum in tow.

"I've never been to a sleepover before!"
said CherryTail.

"I haven't either," said TinyTail.
"I'm a bit nervous!"

"It's going to be perfect!" said StarTail.
"And it's such a lovely day, why don't
we put up a tent outside?"

Shine, Boo, and Yum were so delighted with this idea
that they whirled around in circles
while the FurFins got to work.

It wasn't as easy as they thought, and they got in a terrible tangle!

Just then StarTail's new friend RubyTail arrived with her seahorse Red.
She started laughing when she saw what a pickle they were in.

"Here,
let me help—
I'm good at putting
up tents!"

Soon it was done.

"Teamwork, that's what it takes!" said StarTail,
beaming as she admired the cozy tent. It was decorated
with spring flowers picked by the seahorses.

"I hope Ms. Pearl can make it," she added.
"I sent her an invitation yesterday."

Ms. Pearl was a great big hug of an octopus, and she always
had a cuddle to spare for the FurFins. The sleepover
would be even better with her there.

Now that they'd put up the tent, the real fun could begin.

First, they needed to organize the feast for later. CherryTail was in charge. She was famous throughout Coralia for her delicious cupcakes.

"We'll all come and help, CherryTail," said StarTail.

CherryTail's friends made a terrible mess in her café kitchen,
and RubyTail kept eating the cake mixture—but soon
there was a basket brimming with yummy treats.

They carried it home together, already looking
forward to enjoying the cakes that night.

Back at the tent, RubyTail wondered what they should do next.
"I know," said StarTail. "Let's make friendship bracelets,
and then we can play a game!"

Soon they each had a colorful bracelet—pink for StarTail,
blue for TinyTail, green for CherryTail,
and red for RubyTail.

And none of them could stop laughing when they played musical statues.
They all had to freeze when the music stopped,
but RubyTail just couldn't keep still.

"You'll never win at this!"
TinyTail giggled.

They were having so much fun that they hardly noticed it getting dark.
It was time for their midnight feast of cupcakes.

"Mmm . . . delicious!"
said StarTail.

With warm stomachs, they climbed into their sleeping bags,
excited to be inside their cozy tent.

"This is the best sleepover ever!" RubyTail grinned.

But not everyone was quite as happy . . .

StarTail felt sad that Ms. Pearl hadn't come.

"Don't worry, StarTail," said TinyTail.
"I'm sure Ms. Pearl will be here next time."

StarTail nodded, feeling better, and soon
they were all yawning and ready for sleep.

It was a dark night and the moon was hidden. The FurFins tossed and turned, but none of them could get to sleep.

"Can we turn on the light?" asked TinyTail, who was feeling a bit spooked.

StarTail shuddered. "I can hear something coming!"

Suddenly they saw . . .

. . . a big SHADOW outside the tent!

The four of them held hands tight.
"What IS that?" whispered RubyTail.

"I don't know!" squealed CherryTail,
"but it's getting CLOSER!"

Just then the tent flap opened . . .

. . . and in came Ms. Pearl, carrying
armfuls of sparkly fairy lights.

"MS. PEARL!" shouted StarTail.
"You're here at last!"

"You gave us such a scare!"
said CherryTail.

"I'm so sorry, my lovelies," she said, giving them all a great big octo-cuddle.
"I wanted you to have these lights for your sleepover.

Not that you need them, of course, because with friends
you know you're never really in the dark!"

The FurFins snuggled down under the covers and watched
the lights twinkle as Ms. Pearl read them a bedtime story.

Soon they happily drifted off to sleep.

Before they knew it, the morning sun was shining down.
"Did you sleep well, my lovelies?" yawned Ms. Pearl.

They all dug into a delicious breakfast and chatted about the
nighttime surprise, until Ms. Pearl said, "It's time for me
to be getting home—but I'll be back to visit soon!"

StarTail gave each of her friends a party bag filled with
treats, and little presents for the seahorses too.

"Thank you, StarTail," said RubyTail.
"I had so much fun!"

And as the sun rose higher over the coral and the water sparkled,
StarTail looked at the friendship bracelet on her wrist
and smiled at her friends.

"That really was the best
sleepover ever!" she said.

Then, with a flick of their tails, the FurFins

set off together on another exciting adventure.

To the wonderful Pari —A. R.

For Lola —A. B.

BLOOMSBURY CHILDREN'S BOOKS
Bloomsbury Publishing Inc., part of Bloomsbury Publishing Plc
1385 Broadway, New York, NY 10018

BLOOMSBURY, BLOOMSBURY CHILDREN'S BOOKS, and the Diana logo are trademarks of Bloomsbury Publishing Plc

First published in Great Britain in April 2022 by Bloomsbury Publishing Plc
Published in the United States of America in April 2022
by Bloomsbury Children's Books

Bloomsbury books may be purchased for business or promotional use.
For information on bulk purchases please contact Macmillan Corporate and Premium Sales Department at specialmarkets@macmillan.com

Library of Congress Cataloging-in-Publication Data
ISBN 978-1-5476-0793-8 (hardcover) • ISBN 978-1-5476-0794-5 (e-book) • ISBN 978-1-5476-0795-2 (e-PDF)
LCCN: 2021026254

Art created with pencil and Adobe Illustrator • Typeset in Old Claude LP • Book design by Goldy Broad
Printed in China by Leo Paper Products, Heshan, Guangdong
2 4 6 8 10 9 7 5 3 1

To find out more about our authors and books visit www.bloomsbury.com and sign up for our newsletters.

The End